MERRY CHRISTMAS

Dot Markers Activity Book

We create our books with great love and care yet mistakes beyond our control can happen in printing, binding and shipping. If you have any questions, comments, concerns, or problems with this book please contact us at: bluejewelbooks@gmail.com.

SANTA

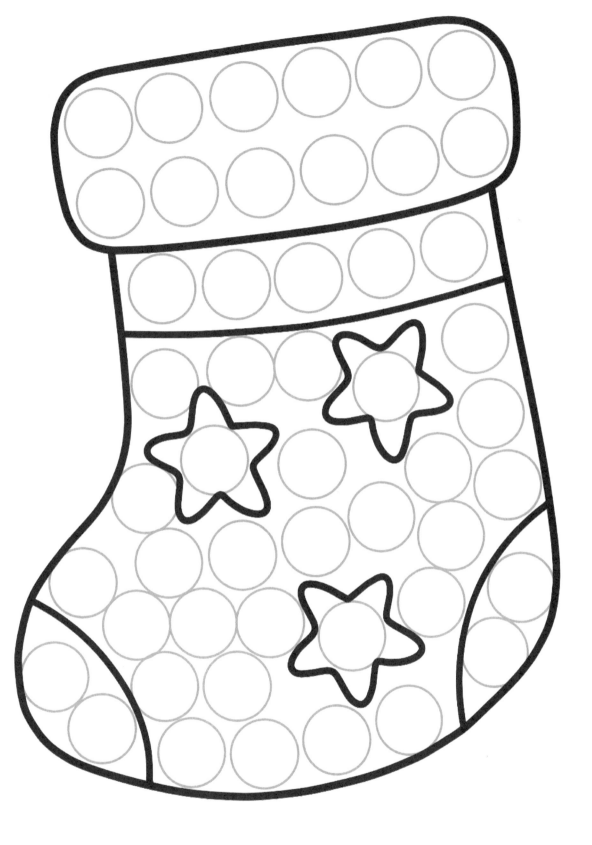

STOCKING

REINDEER

TREE

SNOWFLAKE

BEAR

GINGERBREAD

SWEATER

TRAIN

ORNAMENT

ELF

FOX

CANDY CANE

GINGERBREAD

ICE SKATE

SNOWMAN

TRUCK

WREATH

CANDLE

BELL

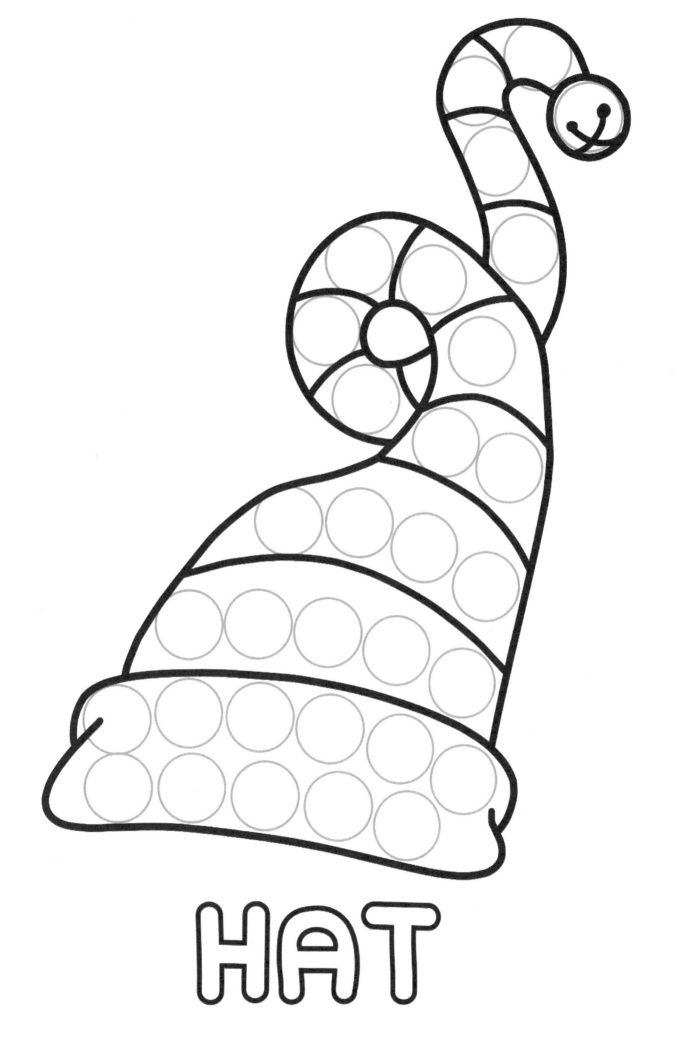

HAT

PENGUIN

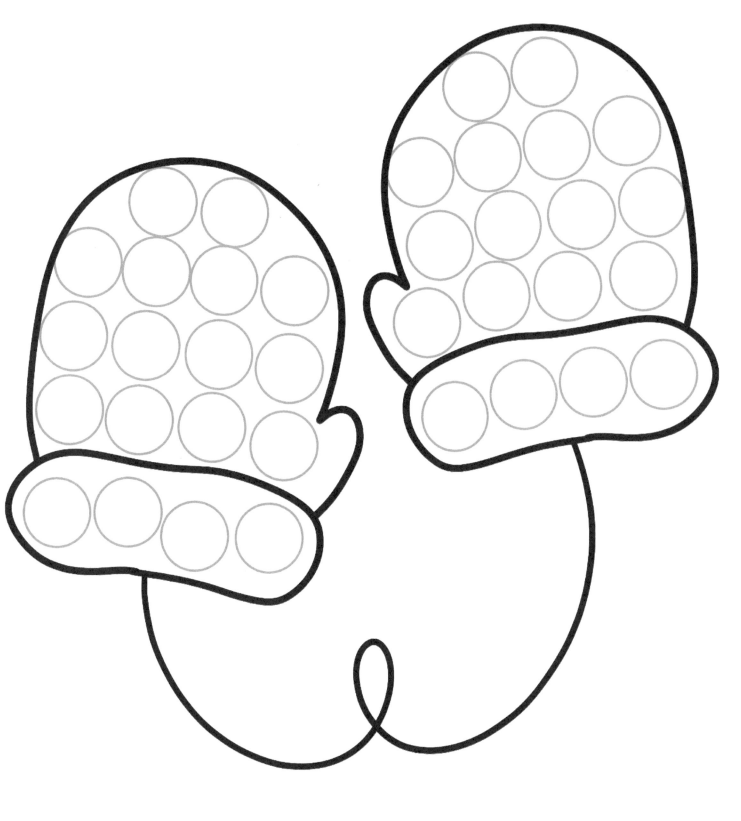

MITTENS

POINSETTIA

CHIMNEY

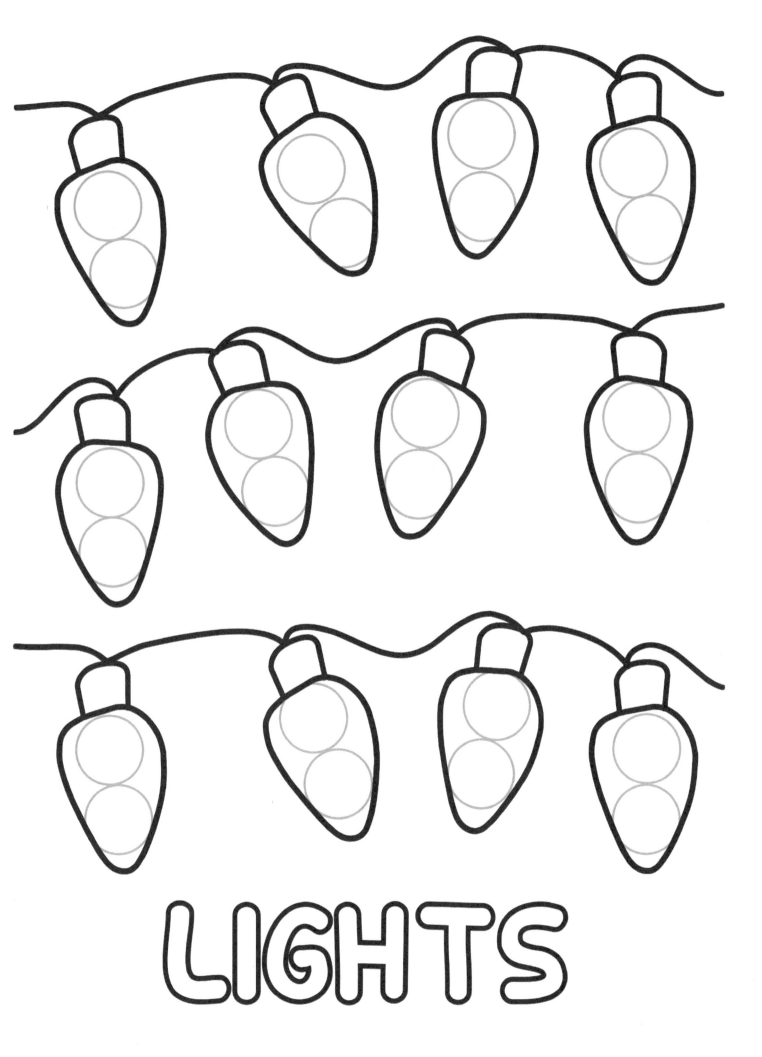

CAT

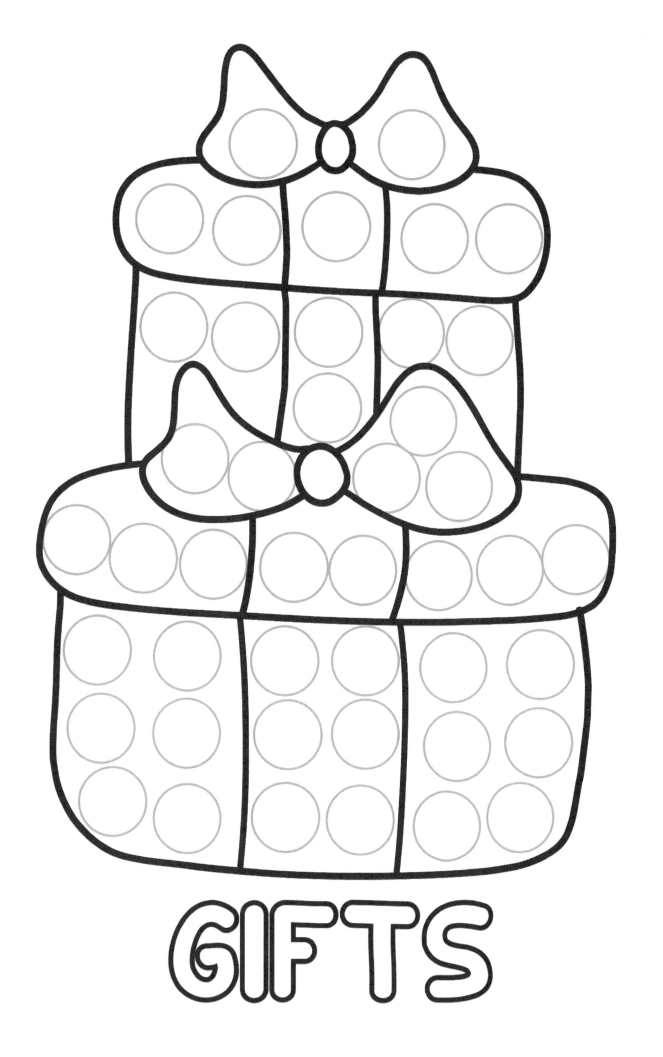

ANGEL

CUPCAKE

SNOWGLOBE

BUNNY

SLEIGH

MISTLETOE

CAKES

DRUM

BEAR

STARS

BIRD

EGGNOG

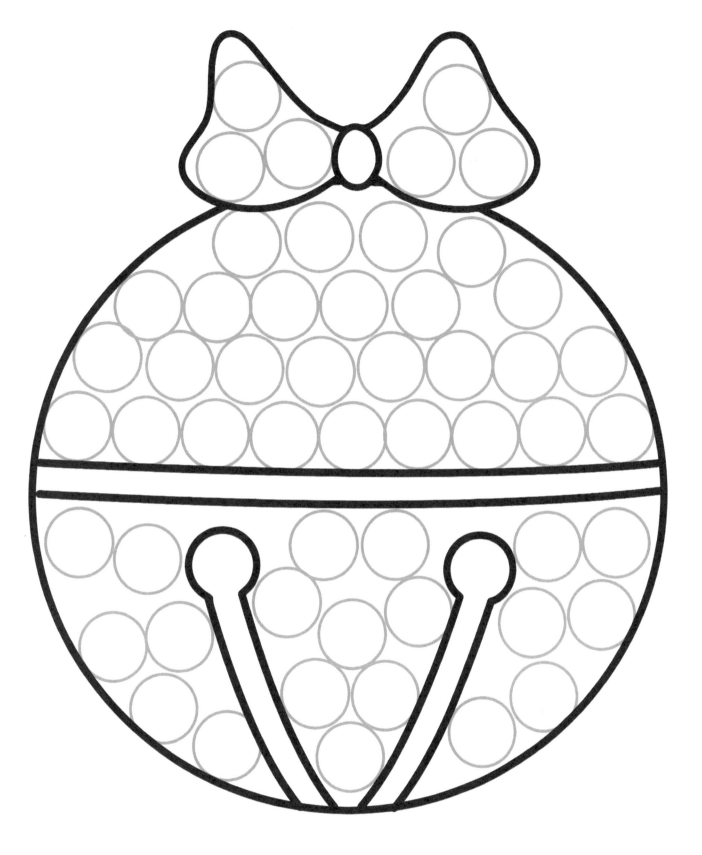

JINGLE BELL

ELF

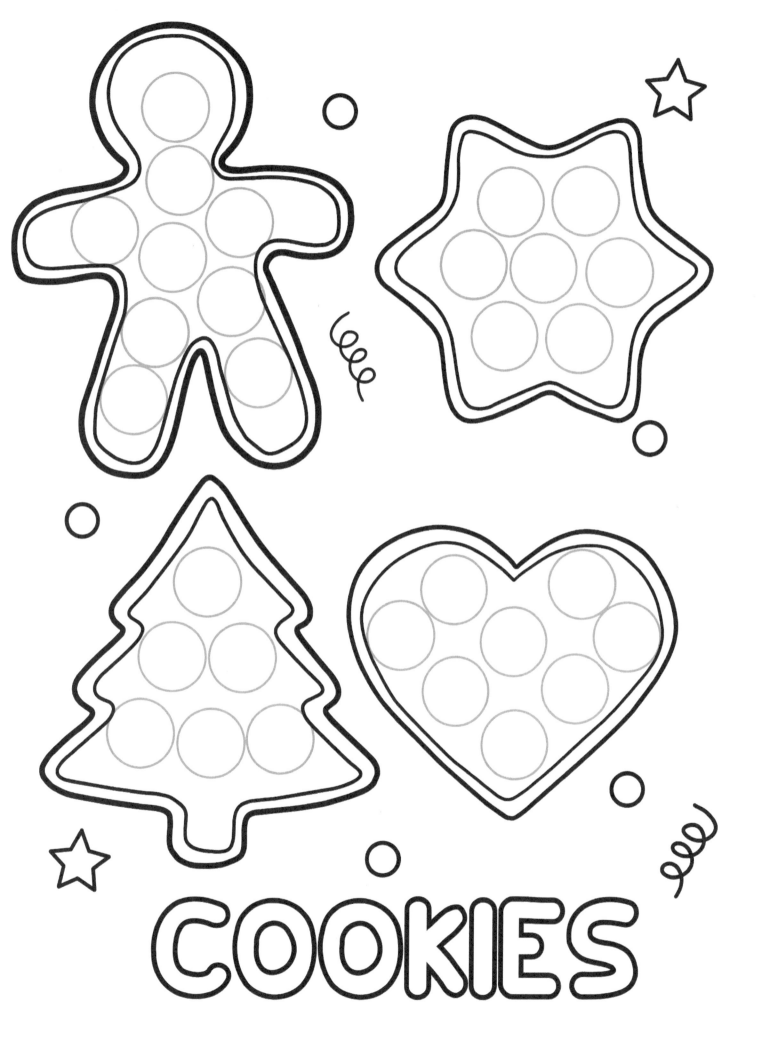

COOKIES

LANTERN

LOLLIPOP

HOLLY

CAR

OWL

ORNAMENTS

SANTA

Made in United States
Troutdale, OR
12/18/2024

26813593R00058